The EYE Book

By Dr. Seuss

writing as
Theo. LeSieg

Illustrated by Roy McKie

HarperCollins *Children's Books*

Trademark of Random House, Inc., HarperCollins Publishers Ltd, Authorised User.

. CONDITIONS OF SALE
The paperback edition of this book is sold subject to the condition that it shall not, by way of
trade or otherwise, be lent, re-sold, hired out or otherwise circulated without the publisher's
prior consent in any form of binding or cover other than that in which it is published and
without a similar condition including this condition being imposed on the subsequent purchaser.

13 15 17 19 20 18 16 14 12

ISBN: 978-0-00-724260-3

© 1968, 1996 by Dr. Seuss Enterprises, L.P. All rights reserved.
A Beginner Book published by arrangement with Random House Inc., New York, USA
First published in Great Britain in 1969.
This edition published in Great Britain in 2008 by HarperCollins Children's Books.

HarperCollins Children's Books is a division of
HarperCollins Publishers Ltd, 1 London Bridge Street
London SE1 9GF

The HarperCollins website address is:
www.harpercollins.co.uk

Printed and bound in China

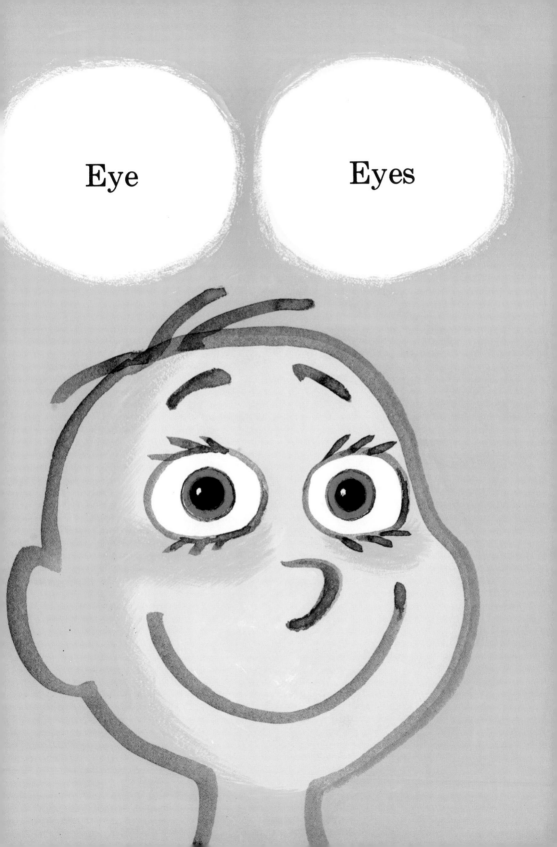

My eyes
My eyes

His eyes
His eyes

Wink eye
Wink eye

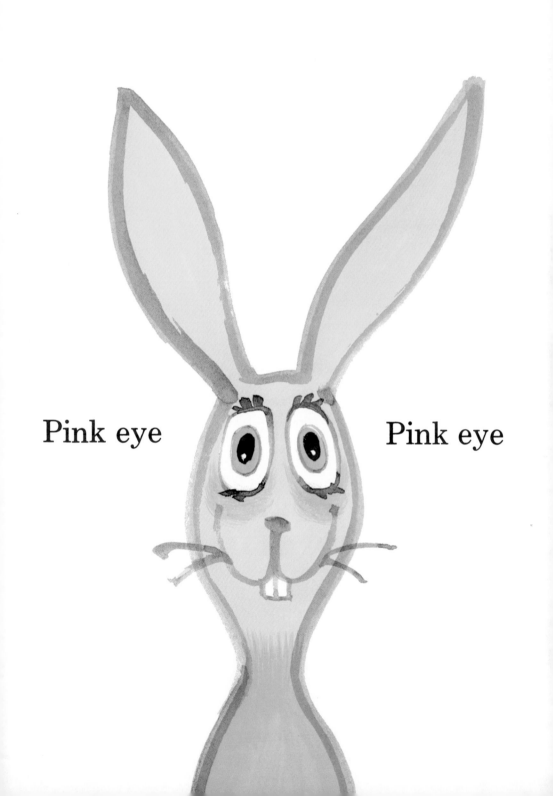

Pink eye   Pink eye

My eyes see.

His eyes see.

I see him.

And he sees me.

Our eyes see blue.

Our eyes see red.

They see a bird.

They see a bed.

They see the sun.

They see the moon.

They see a fork

a knife

a spoon.

They see a girl.

They see a man . . .

a boy

a horse

an old tin can.

They look down holes.

They look up poles.

Our eyes see trees.

They look at clocks.

They look at bees.

They look at socks.

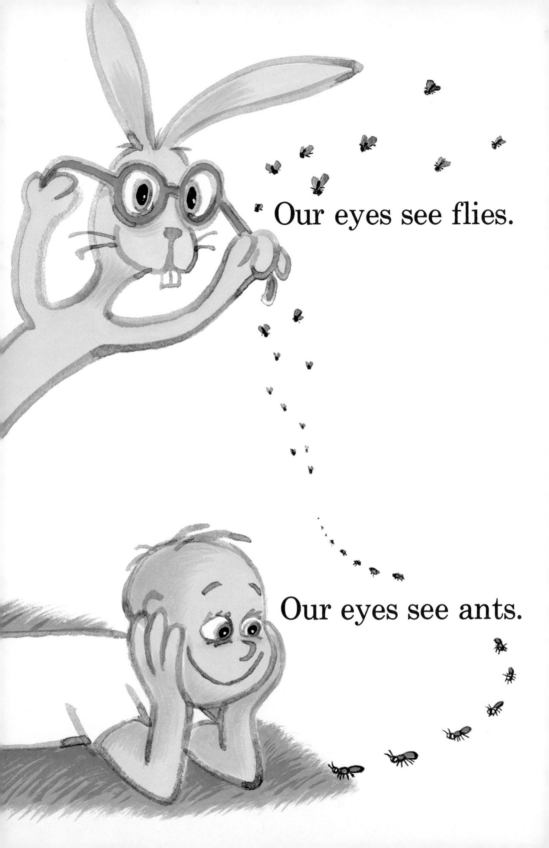

Our eyes see flies.

Our eyes see ants.

Sometimes they see
pink underpants.

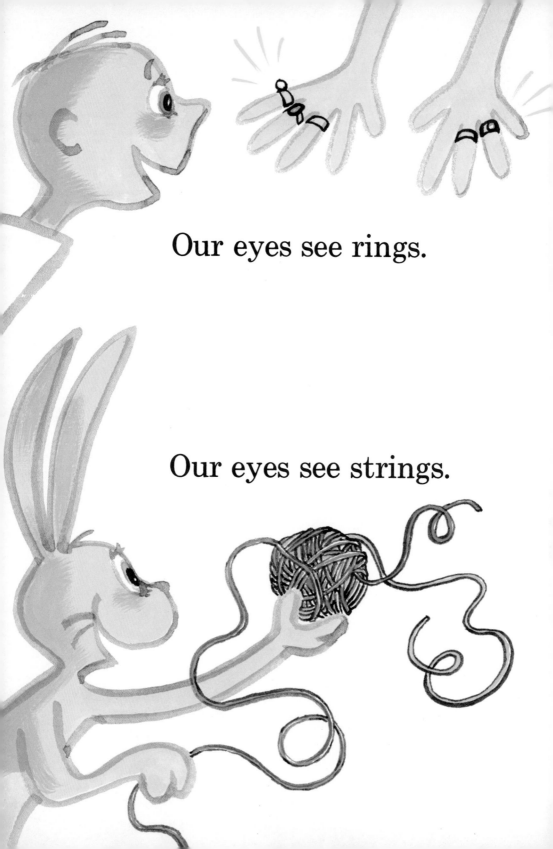

Our eyes see rings.

Our eyes see strings.

They see
so many, many things!

So many things!

Like rain

and pie . . .

and dogs

and aeroplanes
in the sky!

And so we say,
"Hooray for eyes!
Hooray, hooray, hooray . . .

. . . for eyes!"

Read them **together**, read them **alone**, read them **aloud** and make **reading fun!**
With over **50 wacky stories** to choose from, now it's **easier** than **ever** to find the
right **Dr. Seuss** books for your child – just let the **back cover colour** guide you!

Here's a great selection to choose from:

Blue back books
for sharing with your child

Dr. Seuss's ABC
A Fly Went By
The Bears' Picnic
The Bike Lesson
The Eye Book
The Foot Book
Go, Dog, Go!
Hop on Pop
I'll Teach My Dog 100 Words
Inside Outside Upside Down
Mr. Brown Can Moo! Can You?
One Fish, Two Fish, Red Fish, Blue Fish
The Shape of Me and Other Stuff
There's a Wocket in my Pocket!

Green back books
for children just beginning to read on their own

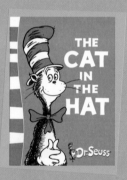

A Fish Out of Water
And to Think That I Saw It on Mulberry Street
Are You My Mother?
The Bears' Holiday
Bears On Wheels
The Best Nest
The Cat in the Hat
The Cat in the Hat Comes Back
Come Over To My House
The Digging-est Dog
Fox in Socks
Gerald McBoing Boing
Green Eggs and Ham
Happy Birthday to YOU
Hunches in Bunches
I Can Read With My Eyes Shut!
I Wish That I Had Duck Feet
Marvin K. Mooney Will You Please Go Now!
Oh, Say Can You Say?
Oh, the Thinks You Can Think!
Ten Apples Up on Top
Wacky Wednesday

Yellow back books
for fluent readers to enjoy

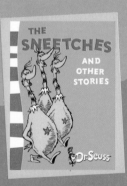

The 500 Hats of Bartholomew Cubbins
Daisy-Head Mayzie
Did I Ever Tell You How Lucky You Are?
Dr. Seuss's Sleep Book
Horton Hatches the Egg
Horton Hears a Who!
How the Grinch Stole Christmas!
If I Ran the Circus
If I Ran the Zoo
I Had Trouble in Getting to Solla Sollew
The Lorax
McElligot's Pool
Oh, the Places You'll Go!
On Beyond Zebra
Scrambled Eggs Super!
The Sneetches and other stories
Thidwick the Big-Hearted Moose
Yertle the Turtle and other stories